17.

MONSTER DAY at WORK

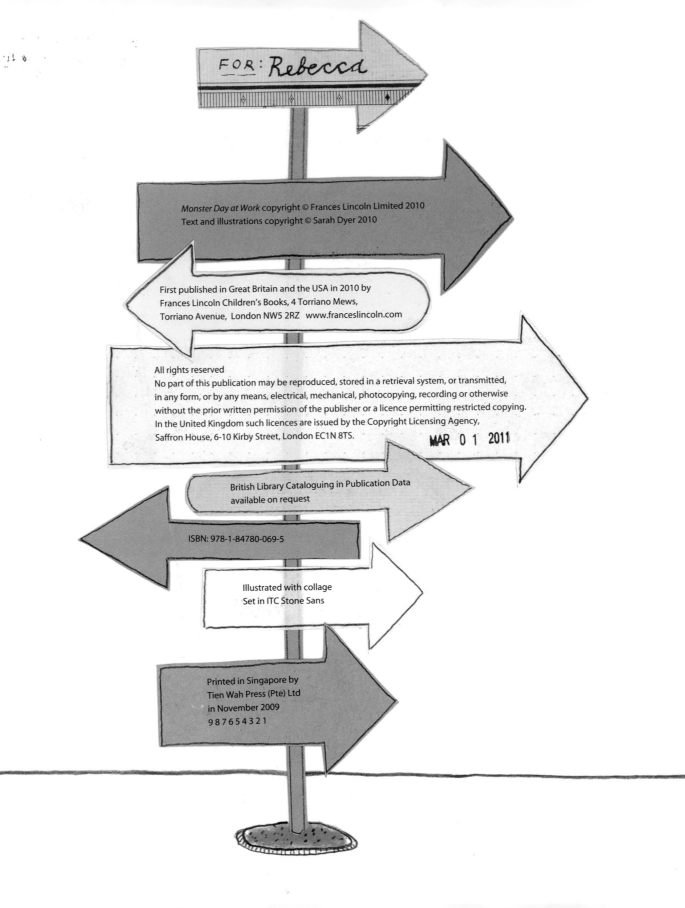

FOR: Rebecca

First published in Great Britain and the USA in 2010 by
Frances Lincoln Children's Books, 4 Torriano Mews,
Torriano Avenue, London NW5 2RZ www.franceslincoln.com

MAR 0 1 2011

British Library Cataloguing in Publication Data
available on request

ISBN: 978-1-84780-069-5

Illustrated with collage
Set in ITC Stone Sans

Printed in Singapore by
Tien Wah Press (Pte) Ltd
in November 2009
9 8 7 6 5 4 3 2 1

MONSTER DAY at WORK

Sarah Dyer

F
FRANCES LINCOLN
CHILDREN'S BOOKS

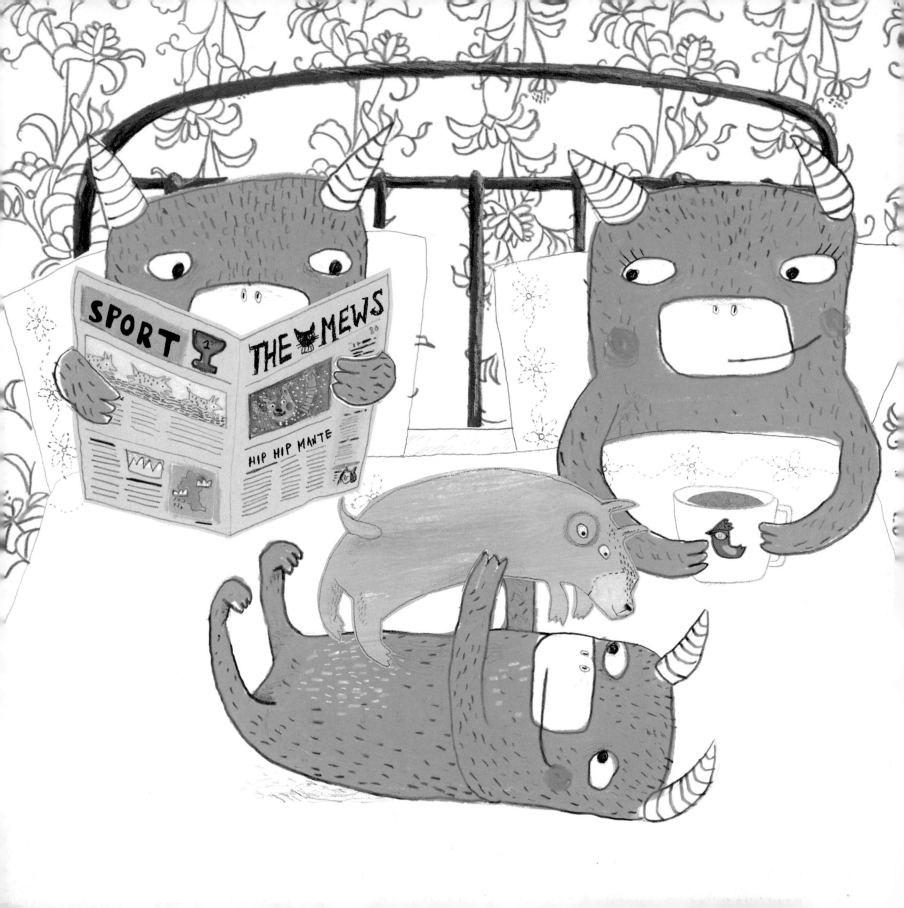

Today Scamp and I are going to work with Dad. I have to do everything Dad does at work.

First I have to decide what to wear.

"Choose me a tie please Scamp.

Ahh . . . lovely choice. Thank you."

Then we have to get to work.

Wow, rush hour really is . . . well, a rush!

The first job is a very important morning meeting.

After the meeting we have to
do some work on the computer.
That is very easy – I get a much
higher score than Dad.

At last it is time for our lunch.

After lunch I colour in the charts Dad has spent all morning working on!

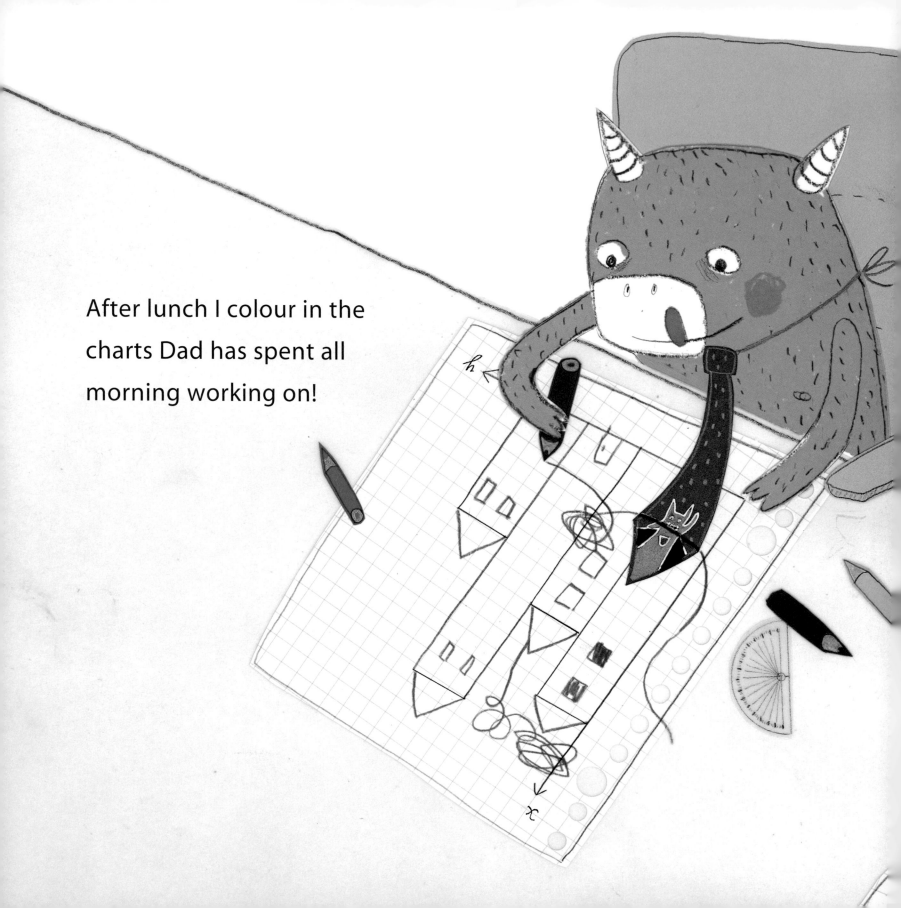

Then we have a nap. Well, I definitely do.

And I'm sure Dad needs one too.

We also visit
the bank.

After work Dad likes to exercise
so we go to the gym.

Then Dad treats me to some drinks.

And Scamp is allowed a biscuit.

Then it is more rush hour on the way home.

I have had a great day. It was all very easy.

I don't know why Dad complains so much,

but I think tomorrow I am going to stay with Mum. . .

Who has it easy too.